Once Upon a Picture

Klee

Renoir

Van Gogh

Rousseau

Sally Swain

ALLEN&UNWIN

Once upon a picture, in 1886,
Pierre-Auguste Renoir painted 'The Umbrellas'.

Now upon a picture we might wonder
about the girl with the hoop.

What does she want to do?

Play?

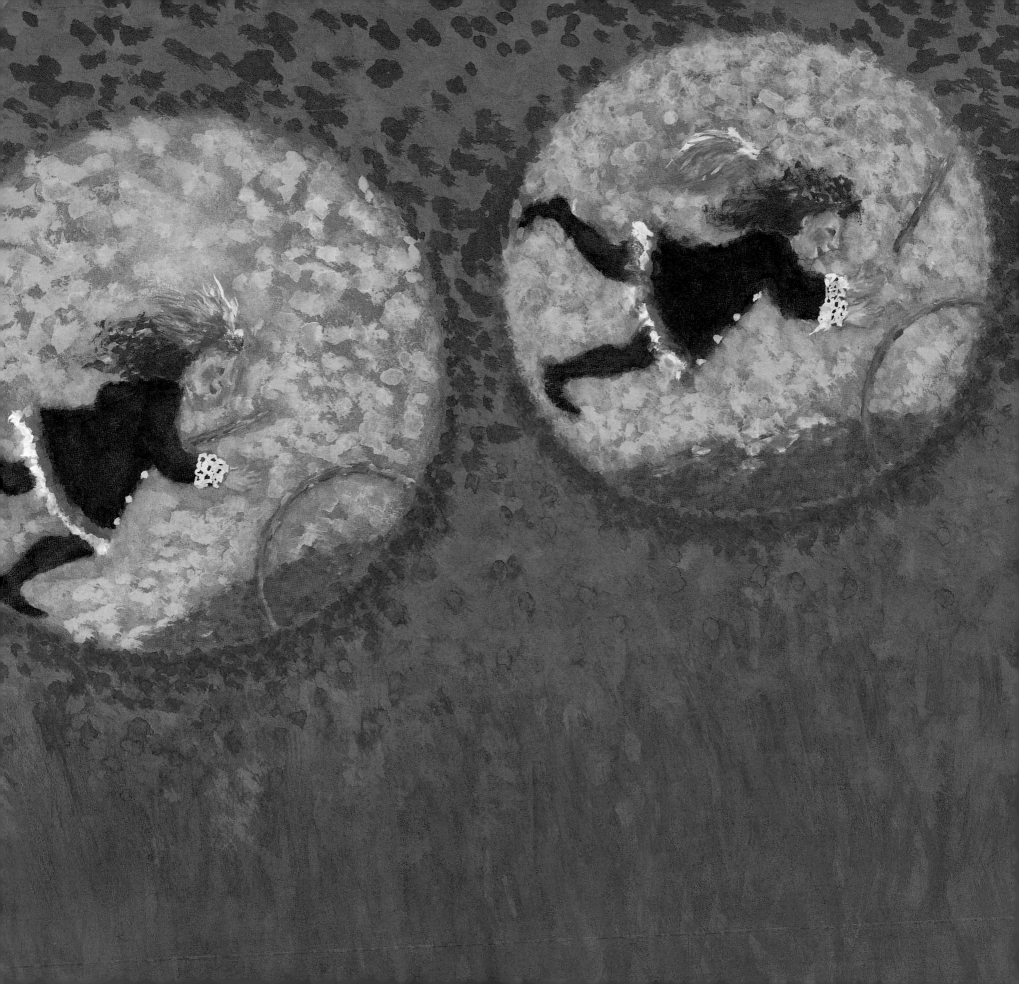

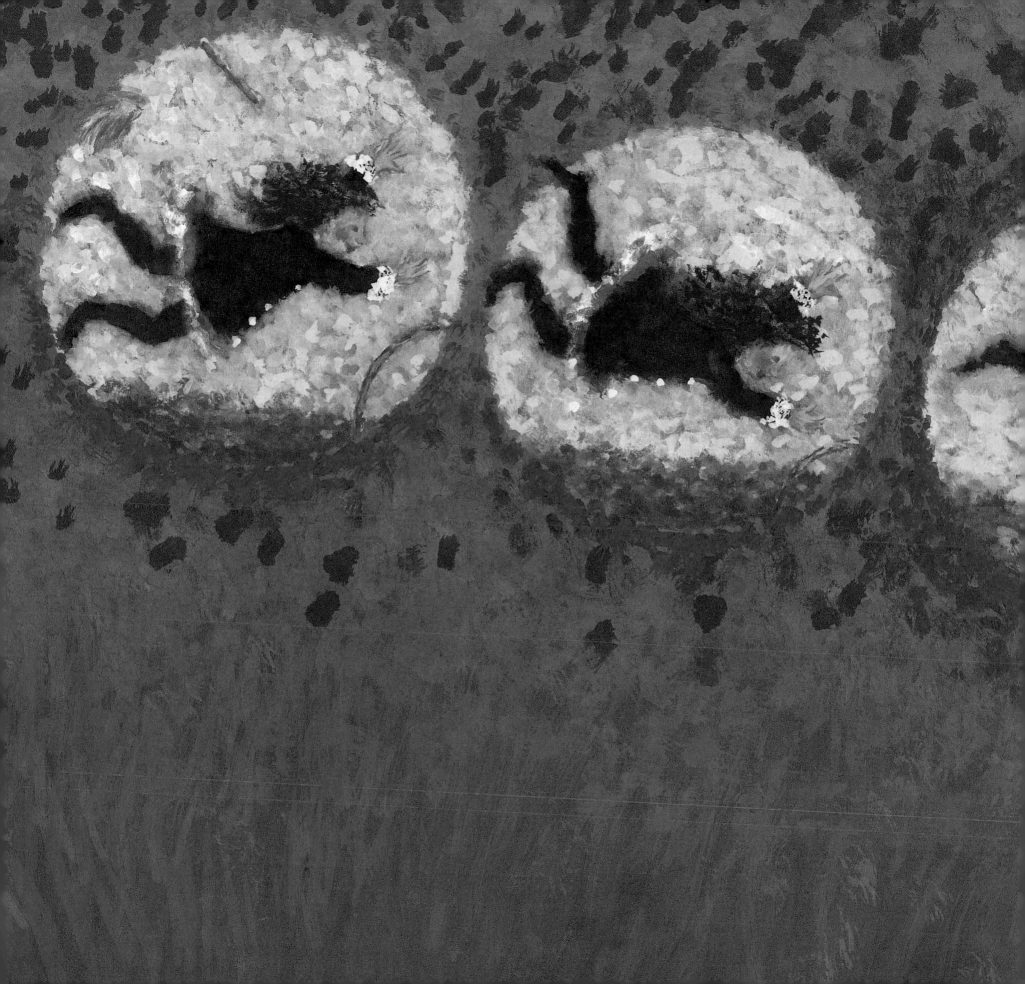

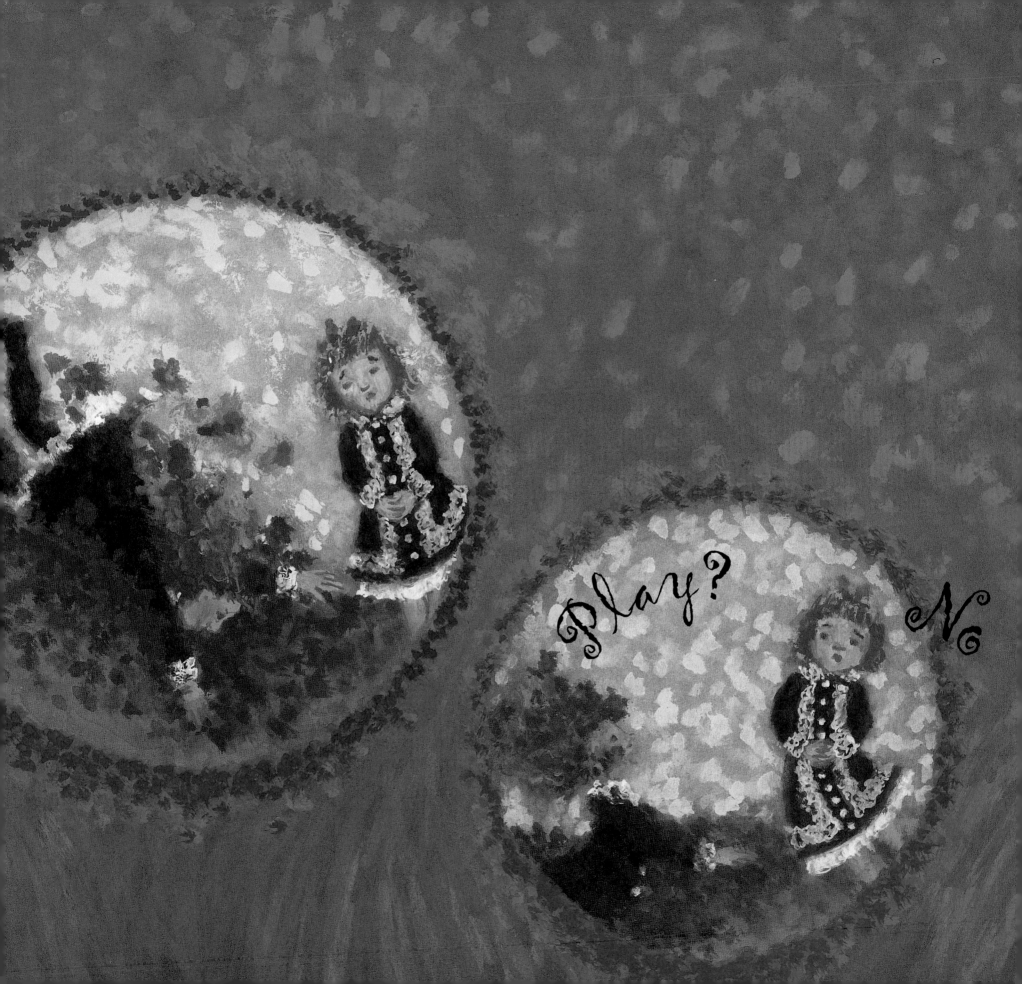

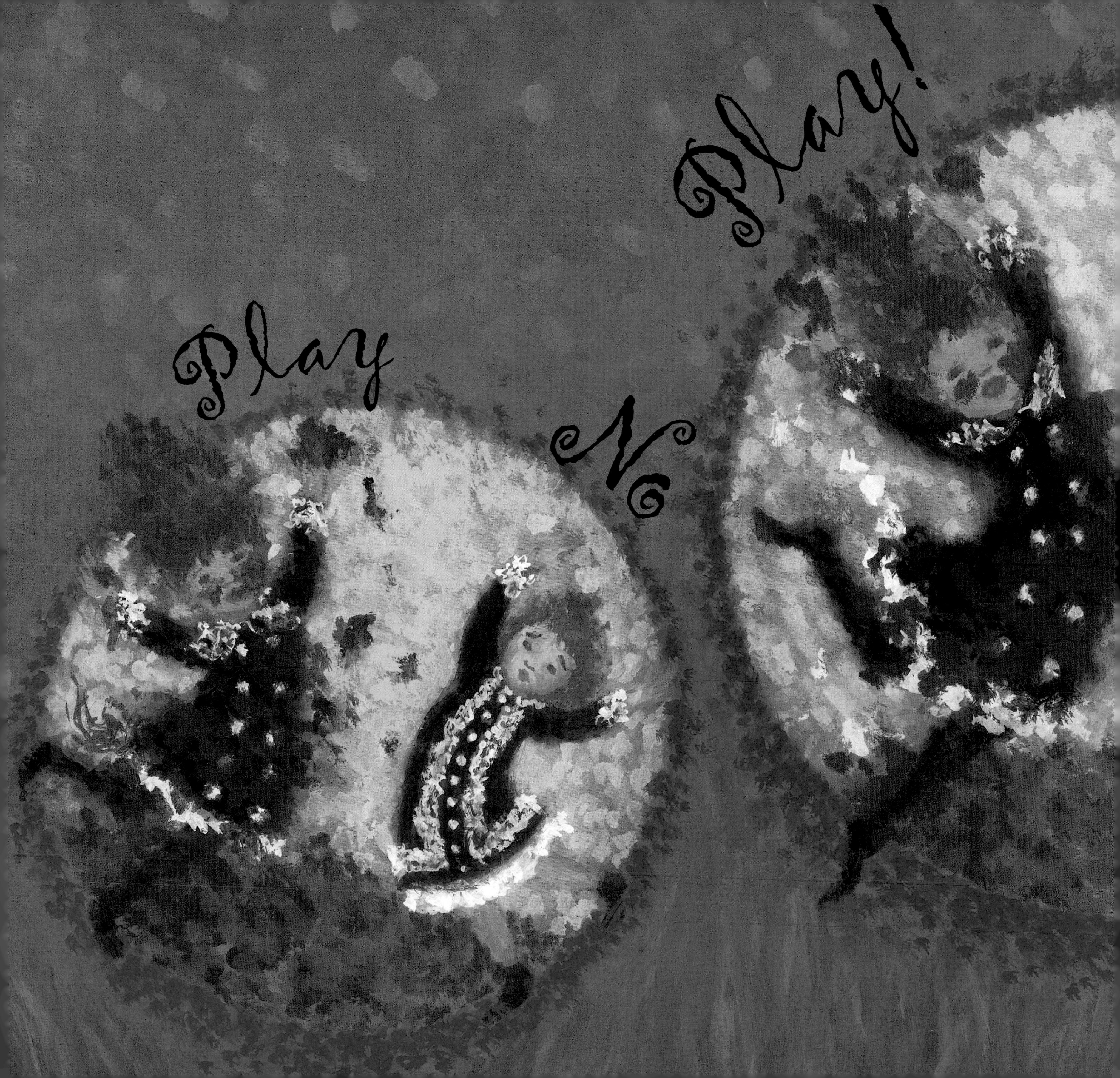
Play
N
Play!

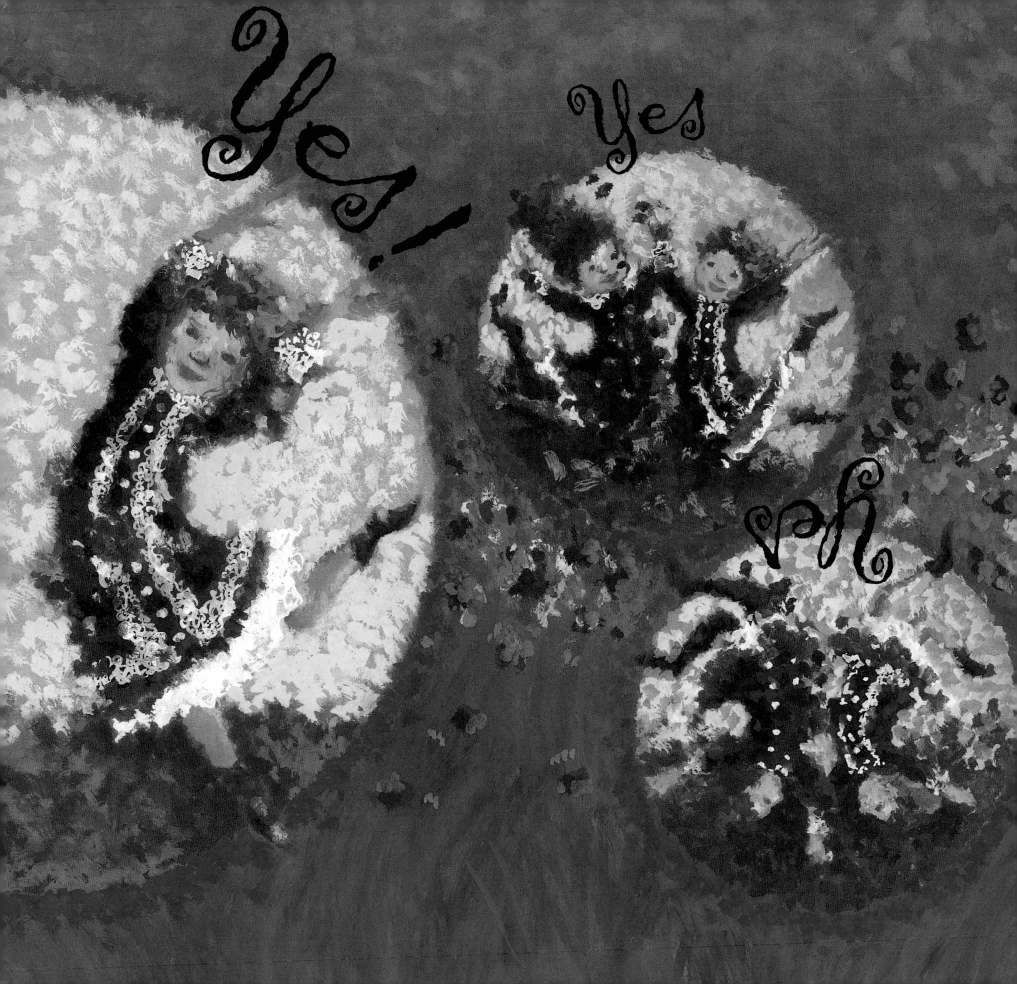

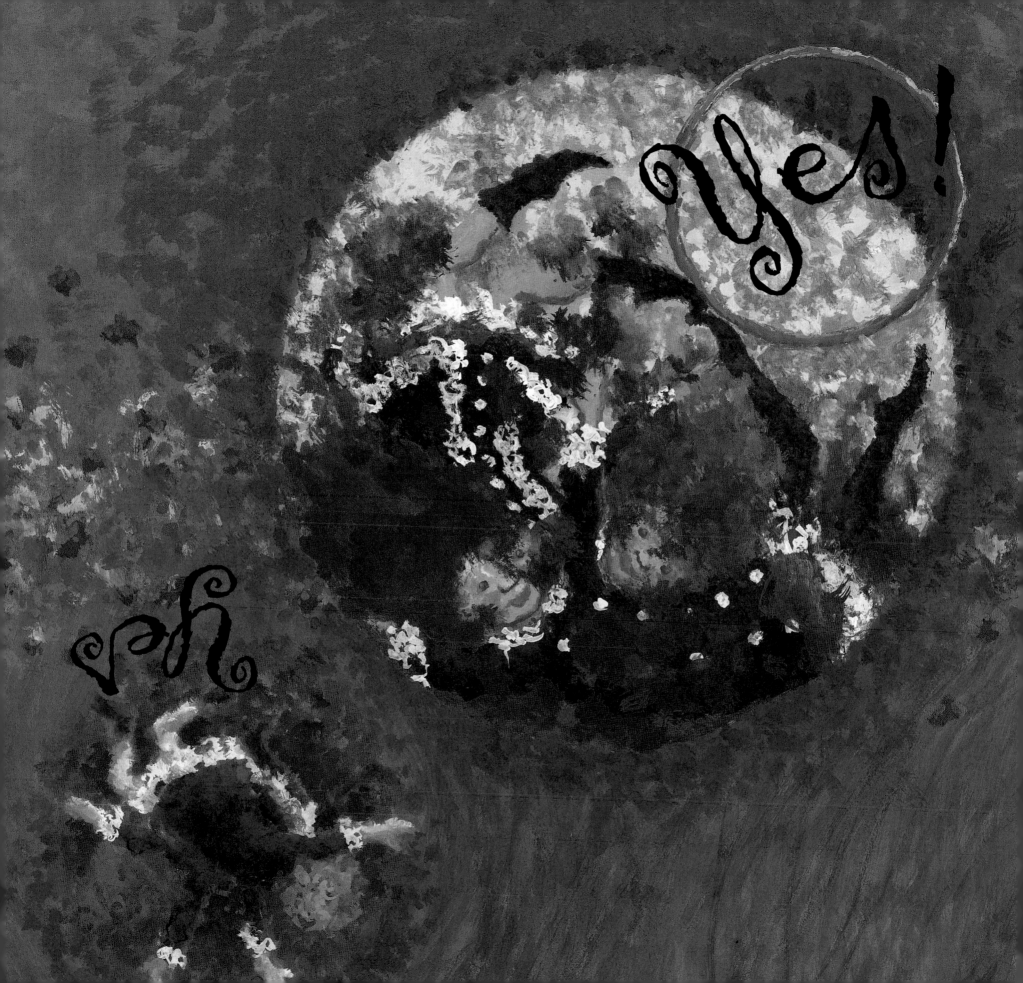

Once upon a picture, in 1922,
Paul Klee painted 'The Twittering Machine'.
Now upon a picture we might wonder
why a machine would twitter.

In the beginning there was a girl who loved a tree...

tweet

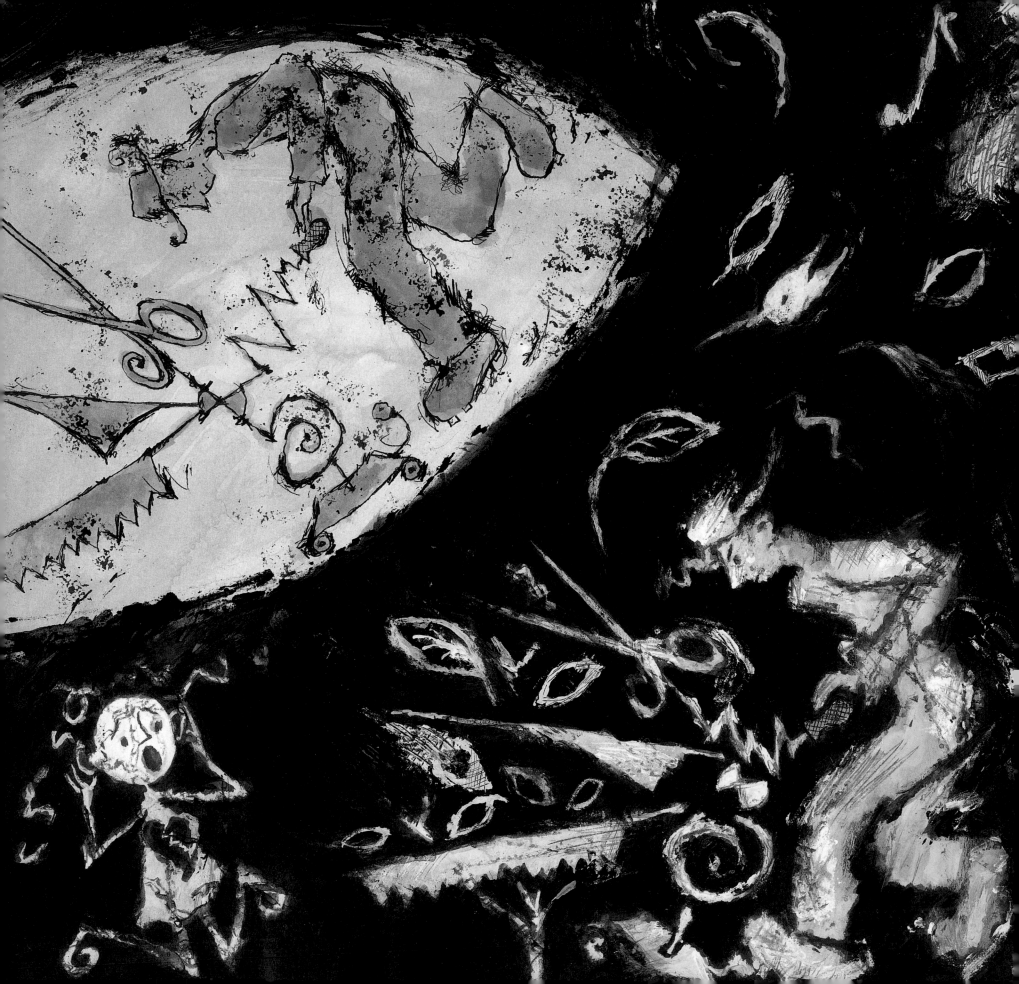

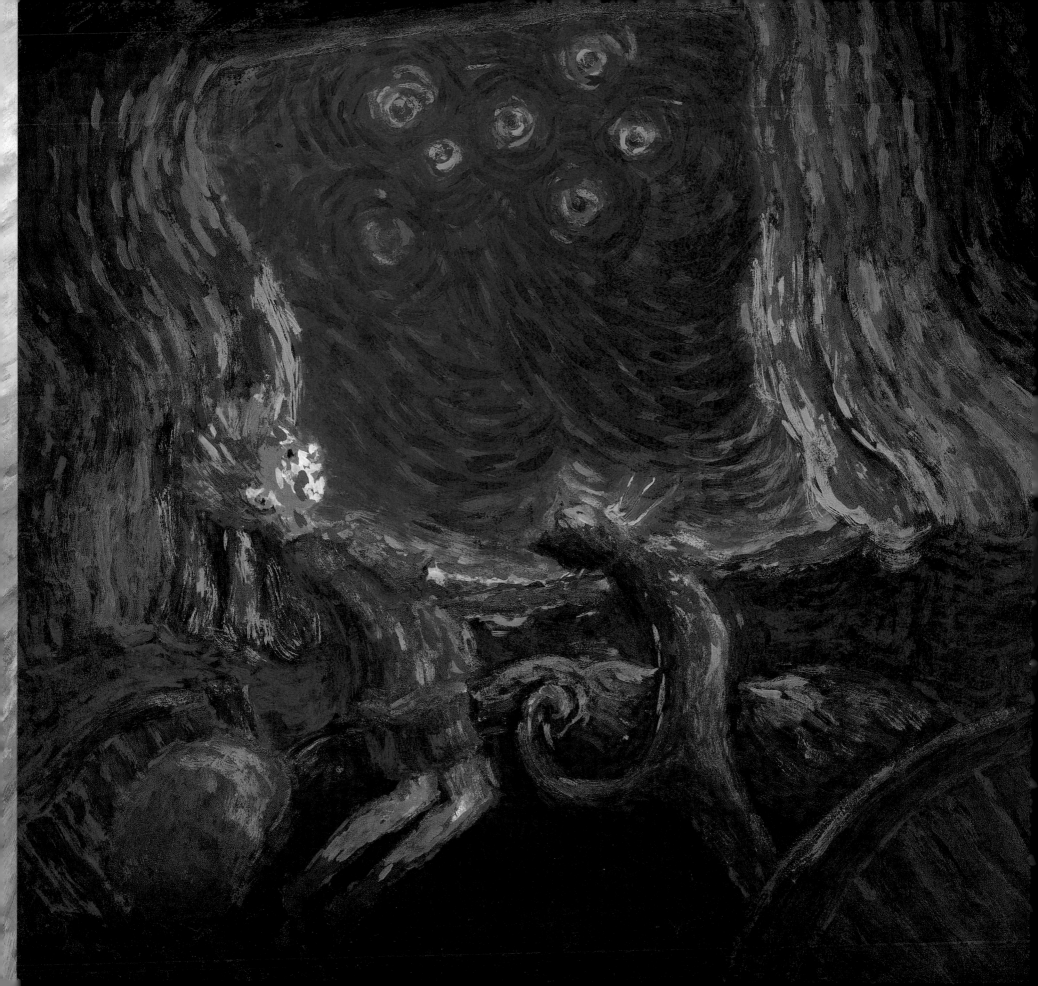

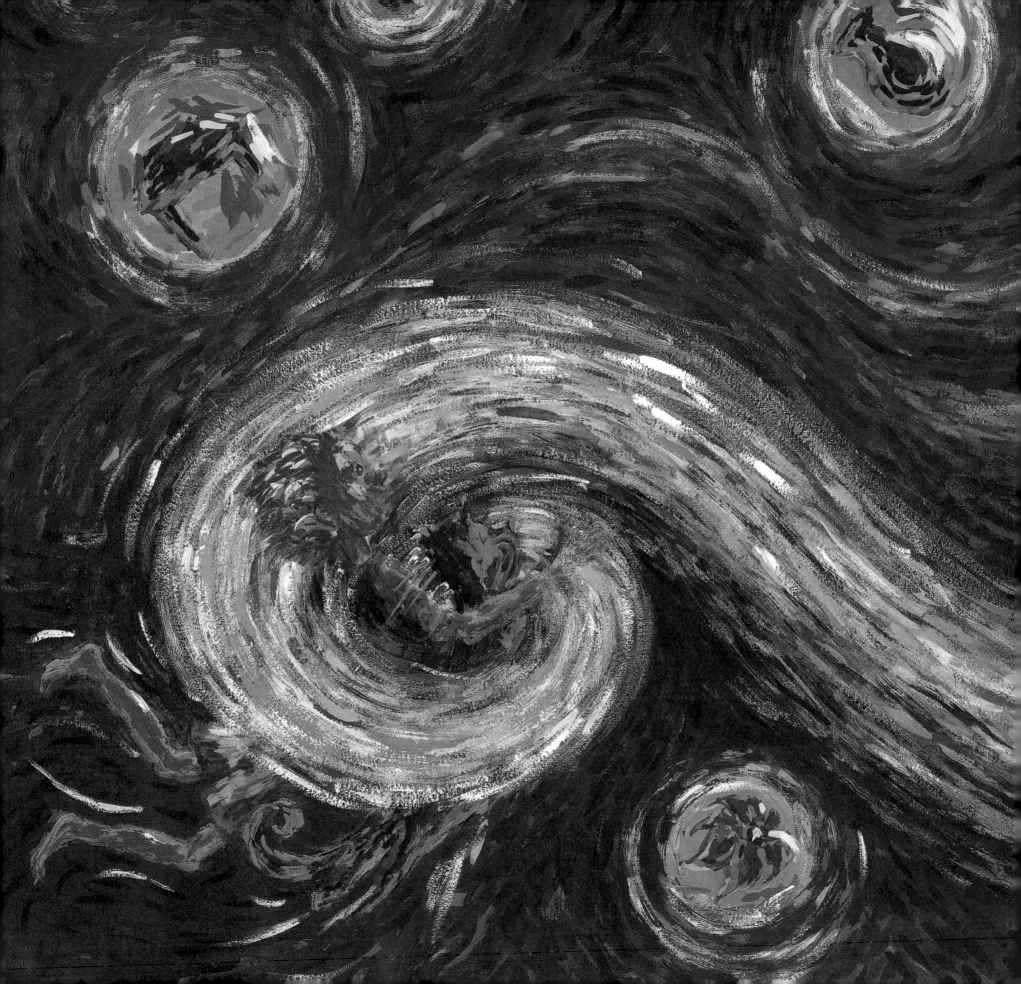

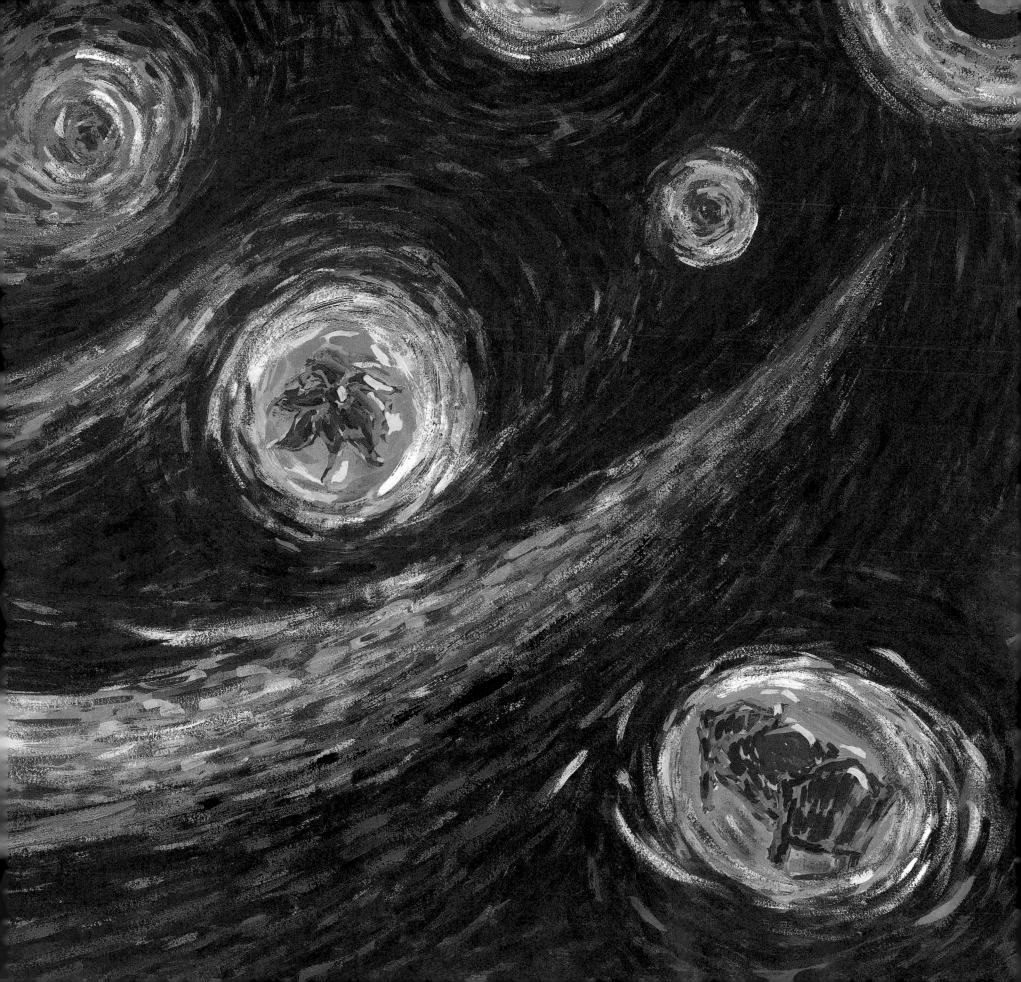

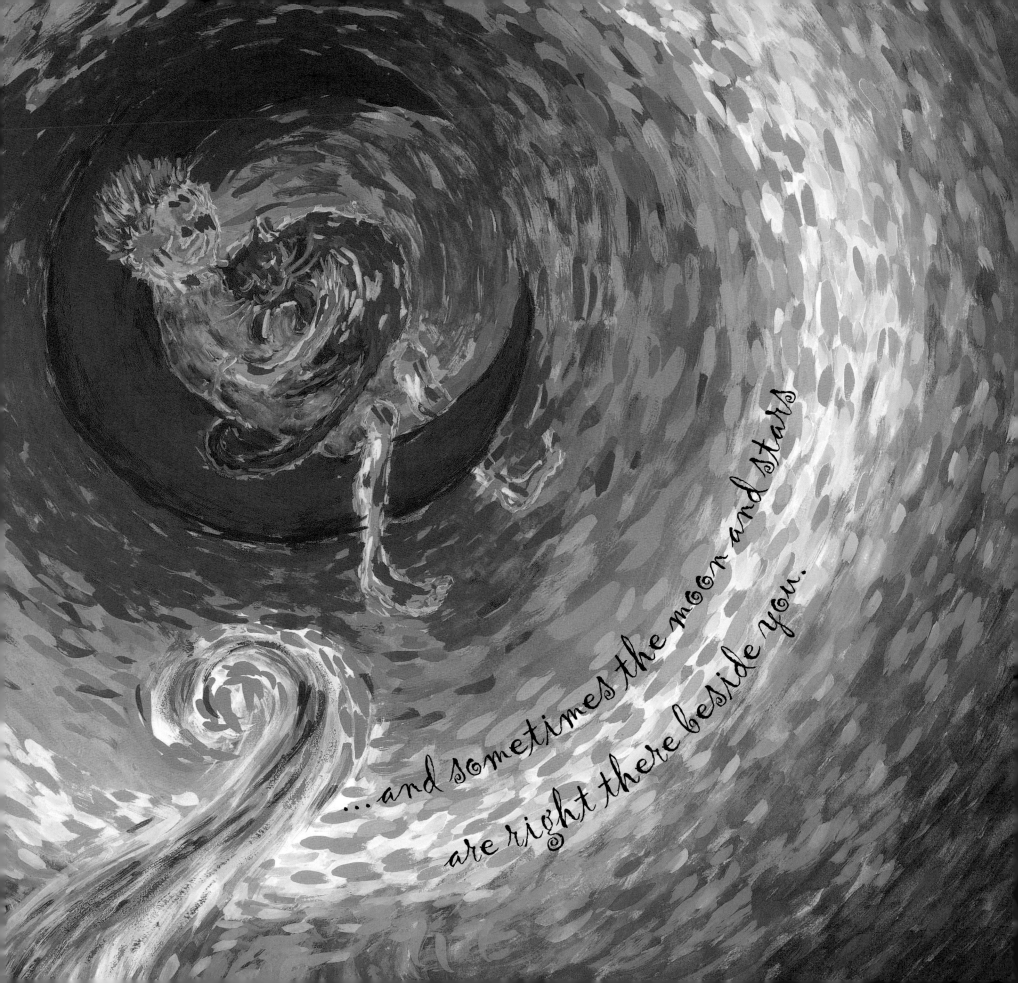

...and sometimes the moon and stars are right there beside you.

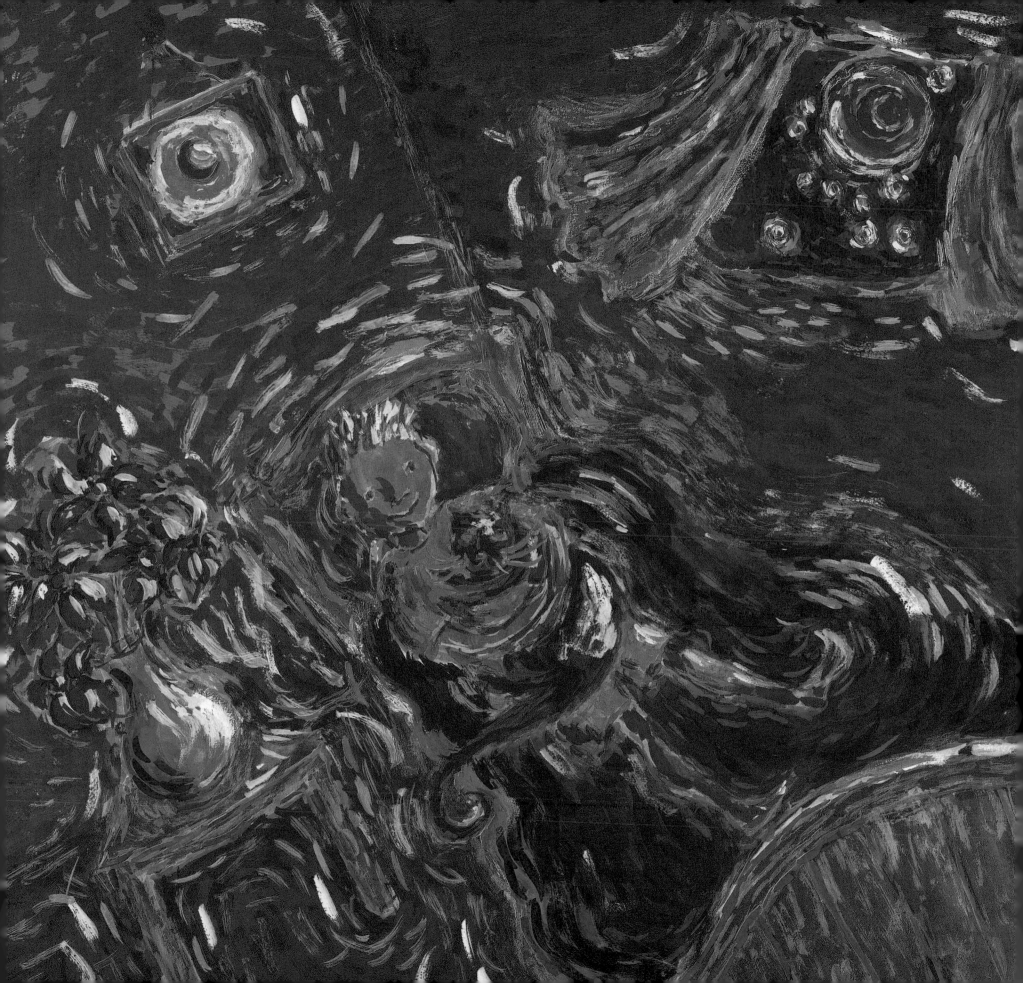

Once upon a picture, in 1891,
Henri Rousseau painted
'Tiger in a Tropical Storm (Surprised!)'.
Now upon a picture we might wonder
why the tiger is surprised.

What makes a tiger a tiger anyway?

Klee

Next upon a picture YOU might wonder...

Van Gogh

Renoir

To Pierre-Auguste Renoir, Paul Klee, Vincent van Gogh and Henri Rousseau:
the Famous Four who provided the essential ingredients

First published in 2004

Allen & Unwin
83 Alexander St
Crows Nest NSW 2065
Australia
Phone: (61 2) 8425 0100
Fax: (61 2) 9906 2218
Email: info@allenandunwin.com
Web: www.allenandunwin.com

National Library of Australia
Cataloguing-in-Publication entry:

Swain, Sally.
Once upon a picture.

For children.
ISBN 1 74114 001 3.

I. Painting - Juvenile fiction. 2. Art - Juvenile fiction.
II. Title.
Cover and text design by Wayne Harris, Monkeyfish
Printed in Singapore by Imago Productions

10 9 8 7 6 5 4 3 2 1

Teachers' notes available from
www.allenandunwin.com

We gratefully acknowledge the copyright holders of the
works of art appearing in this book:

pp 1,2: Pierre-Auguste Renoir, 'The Umbrellas', 1886.
National Gallery, London
© National Gallery Picture Library
pp 1,10: Paul Klee, 'Twittering Machine', 1922.
Museum of Modern Art, New York
© Photo SCALA, Florence, 2002
pp 1,18: Vincent van Gogh, 'The Starry Night', 1889.
Museum of Modern Art, New York
© Photo SCALA, Florence, 2002
pp 1,26: Henri Rousseau, 'Tiger in a Tropical Storm
(Surprised!)', 1891. National Gallery, London
© National Gallery Picture Library
p 32: Pierre-Auguste Renoir, 'Chemin montant dans les
hautes herbes' ('Path Going up through Long Grass'),
c. 1875. © Musee D'Orsay, Paris
Paul Klee, 'The Gold Fish', 1925. © Kunsthalle, Hamburg
Vincent van Gogh, 'Van Gogh's Chair', 1988. National
Gallery, London © National Gallery Picture Library
Henri Rousseau, 'The Sleeping Gypsy', 1897. Museum of
Modern Art, New York © Photo SCALA, Florence, 2002

Acknowledgements

Extra Big Thank You to
Jennie Swain, Stuart Ewings, Iris Swain and David Swain—
the dear ones who loved, looked, listened, tasted,
stirred and said Yes! for the duration of the ten-year
book-cooking period.

Thank you too all friends and colleagues who added to
the deliciousness, in particular —
Erica Wagner, Margaret Connolly, Peter Hall,
Carol Birrell, Jen Keeler-Milne, Liz Gibson, Tony North,
Jane Elworthy, Anita Hansen, Anna Bryan, Janey Kelf,
Sue Atherton, Marg Coutts, Fiona Fitzpatrick, Wayne Harris,
Helen Sanderson and Paper Bag Playback Theatre.